MEMORIES LOST

ALAN CRUISENTINO NICKELSON

iUniverse, Inc.
New York   Bloomington

MEMORIES LOST

iUniverse books may be ordered through booksellers or by contacting:

iUniverse
1663 Liberty Drive
Bloomington, IN 47403
www.iuniverse.com
1-800-Authors (1-800-288-4677)

ISBN: 978-1-4401-8592-2 (pbk)
ISBN: 978-1-4401-8593-9 (ebook)

Printed in the United States of America

iUniverse rev. date: 10/30/2009

This book is dedicated to the only two saints I know on this earth, my two beautiful children, Taya and Tony. I cannot tell you how much joy you have brought to my life, without you I am nothing. I love you both very much! To, Troy and Reg, E., Bobby, Troy B. my Philly Family. My Mother and Father, Thank you for giving me strength and teaching loyalty. Also Alma, the sexiest Bailbondsman of all time! And Keith Ramos, a great friend! And Linden Hagans, the best Attorney on the planet period! And TNT Investigations, the best Investigation company in Colorado period!

Quote from my son,

"Dad, you know what's really cool"? It's so cool that there is the Easter Bunny, the Tooth Fairy and Santa Claus – So you never have to buy anything for us because all you have to do is ask them for what we want and you get it for free so you don't really need money Dad!"

Tony Nickelson
Age 7

CHAPTER ONE

Taya and Tony were more than brother and sister; they were twins, inseparable since birth. The two had always been close growing up together in Philadelphia. Maybe, it was their father leaving when they were two years old, or maybe it was being raised by a single mother who taught them to always look out for each other. Whatever it was, there was a bond between the two that could not be broken or so they thought. Taya was the older of the two, by four minutes, this was a fact that she always seem to remind Tony of, as if he could forget. They had been through a lot together in 17 years and being raised in The City of Brotherly Love, one of the toughest cities in America helped contribute to that. Philadelphia was a dirty dangerous place to live. It had The Projects, (large apartment buildings), drug dealers, prostitution all the qualities that make a city a city. Philadelphia was a city split into sections. South Philly had the Italians and the Italian Mafia run by Frank Sabetti. Southwest had the Blacks and the Junior Black Mafia J.B.M. run by the ruthless Robert Stone. North Philly had the Puerto Ricans and the Latin Kings run by Ben Espinosa. There was an invisible line which separated the cities boroughs and if you crossed that line separating the territories then you paid the price and sometimes with your life. There was always an unsaid respect for the lines which all cultures had and both Taya and Tony had that respect. They were Puerto Ricans and grew up in North Philly where the majority was Puerto Ricans and Dominicans. Their Father was born in Puerto Rico and came to Philadelphia as a teenager where he met their mother, Claudette, a Puerto Rican woman born in Philadelphia. Claudette was a mentally strong woman and she was responsible for teaching Taya and Tony to be equally as strong. Both Taya and Tony Torres were due to graduate in June which was only a month away. Both had plans for a successful life. Taya had gotten accepted to the prestigious Duke University in North Carolina, where her plans were to study law. She wanted to be the first attorney in the Torres Family. Tony had other plans; he was undefeated as an amateur fighter with a record of one hundred three fights with seventy-six of those being knockouts. He had gone to golden gloves three times with three golden gloves wins to show for it. He was a gifted fighter and mild mannered kid, who excelled in mathematics. He hoped to go professional right out of high school and wanted to go to Temple University located in Philadelphia part-time to obtain a degree in Business. Both kids had dreams of finding successful careers, both did not know the future doesn't adhere to plans and sometimes has plans of its own. The Torres children had both acquired enough credits to graduate and both continued to go to school if nothing else but to have fun. All the last minute preparation for the prom, which was a week away. Yearbooks had to get out and

Taya was on the yearbook committee. Taya was a beautiful young Latina girl with black wavy hair that went just past her shoulders on her slender frame. People had always told her that if she didn't make it as an attorney she could always turn to modeling. This was a compliment that she never acknowledged, not that she had anything against models but she always wanted to get ahead using her brains and not her beauty. Taya had just left school it was four o'clock in the afternoon and she was heading to Robert Ray's apartment and she didn't know why. She had broken up with Bobby just two weeks before and ended a tremulous three month courtship because of how he treated her. Tony never cared for Bobby; he didn't believe that Bobby had respect for women. Tony had overheard an argument between Taya and Bobby where Bobby was calling her names on the front porch of their mother's house. Tony was just about to go out there and have a talk of his own with Bobby, but was prevented from doing so by his mother, who told Tony that Taya could take care of this on her own. Tony was glad to hear that the relationship ended. He always felt his sister deserved better. Taya sat on the subway nearing her stop at 30th street station, when she received a phone call from her brother.

"Hey, where ya at?" Tony said.

"I'm on the subway." Taya replied.

"Well do you want me and Carla to pick you up at 40th street? We are still at the gym but we were getting ready to leave and get a couple of strombolis from Falone's"

"No, you don't have to…you guys go." Taya said.

"Why? You have plans or you just like riding on the septa system?" Tony asked.

"No. I'm going over to Bobby's House." Taya said with a slight hesitation.

"What the hell are you doing that for?" Tony asked. Taya could hear Carla in the background asking Tony what was going on. Tony and Carla had met two years before when Carla had moved three doors down from Tony and Taya's home. Tony had never seen anyone so beautiful before, almost like she had a glow. Carla was Puerto Rican with long, black curly hair. Butterscotch skin color. Tony had spoken to her a few times in the past trying to spark up some kind of conversation but Carla would never say much more than "Hi" to him. That changed on the day she was having an argument with her then boyfriend Shawn in front of her home. Tony was just getting home from school and asked Carla if there was a problem. There must have been something that Shawn saw in Tony s eyes because without saying anything further, he left, never ever calling Carla again. That day Carla said thank you and the two began to talk and had been inseparable ever since. They did everything together and Carla enjoyed watching Tony workout at the gym and sometimes working out with him. Taya heard Tony muffle the phone and answer Carla.

"She is going to see Bobby." Tony said with disdain in his voice. Taya could here Carla's reply.

"Why is she…?"

"I don't know." Tony said getting back to the conversation with his sister.

"Listen, he just wants to talk. That's all." Taya stated.

"Well let him talk to a psychiatrist, don't go to his house Tay, you know how he is." Tony said caringly.

"Look, stop worrying, he was crying earlier and even though it's over. It doesn't mean that I have to hate him."

"Nobody said that you have to hate him Tay, but you don't have to meet him at his house. Why don't you meet him at a park or something?" Tony replied.

"Ok, look, you and Carla can pick me up from there ok? I just want to make sure he's alright."

Taya could here the disapproving tone in Tony's voice.

"Okay. We will meet you there." Tony said.

Tony put his right hand up to his mouth and pulled the string to his glove with his teeth. Carla grabbed his other hand and pulled the other pulling the glove off.

"I am going to shower real quick."

"Okay, I will pack up." Carla replied.

Taya was already on the 13 trolley heading over to Bobby's. Bobby was nineteen years old and his own small one bedroom apartment on the Southside. Bobby worked fulltime doing building maintenance for the building he lived and trying to put away money to start college in the fall. Taya had gotten off the trolley at 43rd and Chester Avenue. Bobby's building was located about twenty feet from where she got off. Taya looked up at Bobby's apartment window which was on the second floor of the building. Taya went into the apartment building through the double doors that were suppose to be locked but never were. She went upstairs to the second floor and knocked on the door.

Meanwhile, Tony and Carla were in Tony's car heading over to Bobby's place.

"So tell me the plan again." Carla said with a smile.

"Car, I have told you this a million times."

"Well tell me again, I like hearing it."

"Okay." Tony says giving in. "I go professional in September; fight a few fights working my way up to a championship. You'll be in college studying to be a doctor, and then we will get married right before you start medical school, by then I will be super middle weight champion of the world and then I will pay for medical school outright." Tony said surely.

"So what are you going to after you accomplish all of that?" Carla asked.

"Then I'm going to retire at the ripe old age of twenty-five and them I will be a stay at home Dad." Tony said with a slight grin.

"A stay at home Dad, huh? I never heard that part of the story before. So who are you going to be a dad to because I'm not having any kids until after medical school?" Carla stated.

"Groupies." Tony stated proudly.

"Groupies?" Carla asked

"Yeah, groupies, fans what ever you want to call them." Tony said smiling.

Carla punched Tony in the arm and laughed.

"I got your groupies right here."

"I'm only kidding. You're the only groupie for me." Tony said.

"I'd better be." Carla said smiling.

Carla looked at Tony and became serious. Tony had stopped at a light when Carla turned his face to meet hers and said,

"Tony, do you believe born to be with another." Carla asked.

"I never thought about it to be honest…until I met you. Now every time I go to sleep every dream has you in it. even the dumbest dreams like me walking to the store or something. It's hard to explain." Tony said.

"I think I was born to be with you, and I think you were born to be with me." Carla lifted her hand and put it on Tony's cheek. "I can't picture life without you."

"You are truly my life Carla, I promise you forever." Tony said intently.

Tony arrived at 43rd and Chester Avenue, he could see Bobby's apartment window. He pulled the car over to Parallel Park across the street. Tony looked up to see if he could see anything but he couldn't. It was almost sundown and the sun was reflecting off the windows.

"Can you see anything?" Carla asked.

"No." Tony replied while staring.

"Do you think everything is okay?" Carla asked.

"I don't know…I'll go check."

Alright, and tell Taya to hurry up …I'm starving"

"You're always starving." Tony stated with a grin.

Tony got out of the car and went into the building. The building was old, the kind of building where the air conditioners were hanging out of most of the apartment windows. There was trash in the corners of the stairwell. And it always smelled like someone was cooking some kind of meat that Tony wanted no parts of. Tony walked up the stairs to Bobby's apartment and knocked on the door. There was no answer so Tony knocked again.

"Bobby!" Tony said loudly.

Tony knocked a third time and put his ear to the door. Tony could hear movement from inside.

"Bobby…Is Taya here?" Tiny asked.

Tony then heard a muffled scream yell his name.

"TONY!" the voice screamed.

Tony could also hear Bobby's voice say, "Shut up!"

Tony had heard enough. He tried to turn the handle on the door but the door was locked, so Tony backed up and hit the door with his shoulder. It still did not open. He then backed up and kicked the door. Tony heard a voice coming from inside the apartment yell "TONY!!!" And this time he knew for sure it was his sister. Tony kicked the door again and this time it swung open. Tony saw Taya sitting with her knees up to her chest and her hands were gripping the ends of her ripped sweater and she was crying. Tony ran over to her and then Taya screamed "TONY! LOOK OUT!" Tony turned away from Taya to look behind him and saw Bobby charging towards him from behind the now opened door. Bobby ran into Tony with so much force that he could not stop Bobby's momentum. Both, Bobby and Tony flew from the center of Bobby's apartment through the cracked window. Tony had a hold of Bobby's shirt when they both fell to the ground. Tony landing on his back with Bobby on top of him. Tony looked up and saw a girl screaming "Tony, oh my God." He didn't know this girl. All he knew was that he was tired and needed sleep. Tony closed his eyes to the screams.

CHAPTER 2 - AWAKE

Tony's eyes opened and saw an older Hispanic lady sitting in a chair beside his bed. watching TV, he lifted his hand to feel the bandage over his head. The woman watching TV, was no longer doing so; she stood up and pushed the nurse's button on the wall.

"Hi, my son." The woman said with tears in her eyes. "How are you feeling? Are you okay?"

Tony's head was pounding and his lower back just didn't feel like it should but he felt no need to the stranger that sat crying in front of him that. Tony could tell this woman cared about him and not only that but she called him her son so maybe this woman is my Mother, he thought. Tony began to ask himself questions that he couldn't answer, like how old was he, what is his name, where did he live? As he returned to reality he could see that his apparent mother was waiting for some kind of answer to a question that she had asked while he was deep in thought. A nurse came into Tony's room and over to his bed. Tony's Mother moved away to give the nurse some work space.

"Tony?" The nurse asked. "Can you hear me?"

Tony thought to himself, "That must be my name." The nurse stated that the Doctor was on his way. She held up her pointer finger and asked Tony to follow it with his eyes. Which Tony did, then she asked,

"Can you speak?" she asked.

"Yes." Tony replied

"DO you remember what happened?"

"No."

"Are you in pain?"

Although, Tony was in great pain he didn't feel it necessary to tell this woman who he didn't know, nor did he trust.

"No." he replied.

"Do you know who this is?" the nurse said pointing at Claudette as she moved closer to Tony's bed.

"No." Tony said emotionless.

Tony saw that the woman began to cry harder than she once did. He saw the tears, he understood that she was upset – but he felt nothing. For some reason, compassion eluded him. Tony knew he was supposed to feel something but couldn't. He began to think about who he loved, what he feared and he kept coming up with the same answer – "No one – No one at all." The door to the hospital room opened and a Latina girl walked in with long curly hair. She looked at Tony with joy in her eyes and tears. it was Carla.

"Baby are you okay?" She said while touching Tony's face. her hand felt soft and smelled like roses. Tony had no memory of her but thought that she was very attractive. Claudette grabbed Carla's hand and while looking at Tony said,

"I don't think he remembers?"

Carla looked at Claudette and shook her head, as if saying no with no words before looking back at Tony.

"You don't remember me Tony?"

"No."

Carla's eyes began to fill up with water. Her lip began to quiver.

"Tony, don't say that! You remember me, Tony! You're not leaving me." Carla began to get louder. Claudette could see that Carla was losing it. Claudette looked out the window of the room towards the nursing station which was now looking with concern into the as Carla's voice raised louder.

"You promised!" Carla screamed. "You promised!!"

Two nurses now entered the room and began to hold Carla who was now fighting to get back to Tony's bed.

"No!!! You promised!" Carla screamed. Tony's facial expression did not change; he began to think about who he loved, what did he fear? And he kept coming up with the same answer.

"No one – and nothing.

Chapter 3 - Remember

2008, Taya lay in bed, remembering that day that seemed so long ago. She remembered how close she and her brother had been. Taya hadn't seen Tony in about nine years. She thought about how she felt sitting in the hospital with both her mother and Carla when they were both told Tony had brain damage and would never be the same person we remembered. And from that day he wasn't. After bringing him home, Tony just left. He left a note for their Mother which said:

Claudette and Taya,

I am leaving and I will not be back for while. There are things I need to figure out on my own. I apologize for any inconvenience I may have caused. Thank you for all of your help and corporation.

Tony.

The letter was just as cold as Tony had become. She remembered how she felt when she was first told about the career choice that Tony had pursued from a former friend. Troy Martin, who boxed with Tony in the past. Troy had said he heard Tony was a set up man for Frank Sabetti. Taya had never that term before that day but had since learned that a set up man was a person the mob sent in for people they couldn't kill. There were certain people the mafia wanted very much

Wanted to kill nut killing that person would bring too much unwanted attention to the mafia. For this reason the mob would send in a set-up man whose job it was to set up this unwanted individual for a crime that he didn't commit. A good set up man could make a person's life very uncomfortable. A great set up man could have you prosecuted to the fullest extent of the law for a crime you have not committed. Tony from what Taya had heard was a great one. Taya lay in her bed turned on her side looking out at the sun which was beginning to come up in the sky, out in the back yard. She briefly thought how she could use a guy like Tony for this trial which was about to start in a week.

Patrick and Monica Martin, husband and wife had lured a twenty-two year old black man, Tyrone internet with hopes that he found a possible love match with Monica. When he arrived at the party to meet Monica, he was met by Patrick who savagely beat him to death with a sawed-off shot gun which was never found. Taya pondered about how difficult this case was going to be to prosecute. It was a high profile case which drew a lot of media attention. This meant that Taya had a lot of eyes on her, if she wanted to run for some type of office, in the near future. Then the decisions she made today would affect that decision tomorrow. Taya began to run her fingers through her hair while she laid on the pillow looking out the window. She continued to think of Patrick and Monica; she knew she had virtually no evidence except emails between Monica and Tyrone. Only one eye witness who was driving by at the time at the time and whose memory was becoming more questionable by the day. Taya knew that this witness was being intimidated by Patrick and or his white supremacist friend but this was also another fact that Taya was having a hard time proving. Taya had been an assistant DA for three years following Law School and was building a reputation for herself as a prosecutor. And from his reputation she was securing a future for both herself and her husband Mark. She and Mark were both lawyers who met in their First year together at Duke University. They had been together for seven and married for three years. Mark Hagans was criminal defense attorney where as Taya was on the prosecuting side this led to some passion filled debates quite often in the Hagan home. The two may not have always agreed but they did agree on being each others rock. Taya had felt that Mark wasn't the most handsome man in the world, but she knew without a doubt he was the gentlest, caring and responsible man she had ever met in her entire life. These qualities made him attractive and sexy to her, and she knew that when they exchanged vows that this was the man she was destined to share forever with. Taya felt Mark lying behind her. He took her hand from her hair and interlaced both their fingers as he pulled her hand down to her side. She snuggled against him.

"What are you thinking about so hard?" Mark asked

"Nothing – what makes you ask that?" Taya said.

"You only do that to your hair when you're deep in thought or stressed out." Mark said calmly.

Taya didn't want her husband to stress out like she was. She wanted to tell him that Monica Martin had told her to watch her back as she left a Motions Hearing.

She wanted to tell her husband that she knew Patrick and his friends were white supremacist and they were quite known for intimidation of both witnesses and prosecutors in previous cases. Cases that were all thrown out for lack of evidence or because a witness decided to skip court preferring a jail sentence over giving testimony against Patrick and his friends. Taya wanted to tell Mark so many things. Taya wanted to tell Mark so many things but didn't. Taya could feel Mark's excitement growing harder behind as he began to kiss her back through her Victoria's secret silky pink shirt. Mark's hand went slowly up her arm caressing her neck before moving over her breast.

"I see you have a plan to get things off of my mind." Taya said before turning to face her husband. The two began to kiss as they began to make love.

Chapter 4 - "Tony"

Tony stood in the closet located in the spare bedroom of the Ida Herrera's condo. Ida was the girlfriend of Matthew Masso, a local "Friend of Ours" who was now getting under the skin of Frank Sabetti. Matthew wanted to be Frank, controlling the South Philadelphia mob. Mathew had started approaching people who he thought that he could trust with ides for taking over Frank's place. And it wasn't long before these trusted individuals met with Frank and filled him on the plot to replace him. Tony was sent in to make Mathew suffer hell on earth, which was Tony's specialty. Tony had been standing in the closet for about two and a half hours. This is when Mathew and Ida arrived back at the condo from eating dinner at Maggiano's Italian restaurant, as the two did every Wednesday evening. Tony had been following both Ida and Mathew for two months, learning them studying their every move. While doing this he made spare keys of both their vehicles and homes. He had been in the Mathew's home time and time again. Successfully without being detected. As well as Ida's home with the same result. And tonight would be the last time he was in either household. Tony was six feet tall, slender build with a size 11 shoe. Mathew on the other hand was short. Wearing a size nine shoe. Tony had been studying Mathew's size nine shoes for too long and his toes were beginning to throb from the pain. Tony could hear that the couple was done making love and he knew that Mathew would be leaving soon. After all he had a wife to get home to. Tony checked inside Mathew sweat suit jacket pocket that he was currently wearing to make sure the knife that he had gotten from Mathew's trunk was still there, it was. Tony's hands were sweating from still having the surgical gloves that he had put on hours before he had entered the home. The room that Tony chose to wait in was a guest room (an extra room) in the two bedroom condo. Ida had no children nor did she have guest who stayed with her frequently, if at all. The room had minimal furniture, consisting of just a bed and two nightstands. The closet Tony stood in housed all the winter clothes that she would break out in two months. Tony didn't hear the good-bye but he did hear Mathew sneaking down the stairs going to his white Chrysler 300 which was parked under the carport. From the times Tony had been there before he noticed that Mathew would always leave quietly as to not wake Ida up. Tony never understood how Mathew could apparently respect her enough as to not want to wake her, but didn't respect her enough to have a life with her. Only seeing her at night, never taking her any place other than dinner once a week at the same restaurant. Tony took his mind off of thinking about Ida's respect to listen to Mathew's car start up. Once the car started Tony opened the closet door, closed it gently behind him. He could still hear the car warming up as he stepped out of the guest room walking towards the bedroom where Ida laid facing away from him. Tony kneeled on the bed, reached into his pocket pulling out the knife and stabbed Ida through her temple. Her body jolted and twitched but she did not grab Tony, nor could she. She had died instantly. After Ida's body lay still, Tony stabbed her nineteen more times in the chest and the palms of her hands. Tony wrapped Ida's body in the sheets and comforter and carried the small frame woman down the steps to the front door. He opened the curtain on the door slightly, just enough to witness Mathew driving off. Tony pulled a black folded trash bag from his back pocket and stuffed both Ida's body and the bed linen into the bag. Tony had rented am expedition which was parked next to Ida's condo in the non-rented spaces. Tony pushed a button on his keychain opening the hatch of the vehicle from inside Ida's doorway. Tony opened the door and looked around…he saw no one. There were three units which faced Ida's unit, one was vacant and the other two were occupied that is until a couple of days ago when there was a fire which looked to the fire marshal as starting from between the unit walls, forcing it's occupants to make other living arrangements until repairs could be made. This was no????. As Tony left nothing to chance. Tony scanned the area once more before taking Ida's body out to the back of the expedition and closing the hatch. Tony looked at his watch and he knew he didn't have much time. It would take Mathew forty minutes to get home and it would take Tony twenty minutes to make it to the airport where another rental car awaited his arrival at short term parking it was the only place at the airport that didn't have video surveillance.

Tony rushed back inside Ida's home. Once in her bedroom he grabbed a suitcase threw in some clothes both from her drawers and closet. He also grabbed Ida's purse and put that in the suitcase as well. He zipped the suitcase shut and turned off the light to the bedroom, went down the stairs leading to the front door and locked it for the last time. Tony went to Ida's black Kia unlocked it, with the set of keys he had made. Adjusted the seat and drove to the airport. Tony was calm as always. Since his accident he was unable to become nervous, stressed and could not feel fear or sympathy. As Tony drove he thought about perfecting this set-up envisioned the police putting handcuffs on Mathew, he envisioned it he willed it. He arrived at the airport. Received a parking stub and drove in, parking next to a Honda civic he had rented two days ago. Tony got out of the Kia and the seat up, not where Ida would usually leave it, but closer than it had been to a man of Tony's height driving it. Tony walked over to the Honda, unlocked it and opened the glove compartment and retrieved a clear baggy with strands of hair in it. Tony brought the baggy over to the Kia and pulled out a single strand of hair and placed it on the head rest. He took another and placed it on the side of the driver's seat. He then grabbed the suitcase. Tony then locked the car door and went back to the Honda, got in and drove off. He put the parking stub inside the back pocket of the sweat suit he was wearing which belonged to Mathew and zipped it up inside of it. Tony pulled over and popped open the trunk where he had a spare pair of jeans, boots and a t-shirt. He looked around the road was completely empty. He pulled off the sneakers and the sweat suit and threw them into the trunk. While quickly putting on the clothes he had. Tony got back in the car and drove to an apartment complex where there was a dumpster. He threw the sweat suit, sneakers and the suitcase inside it. Tony got back in the car and drove once again back to Ida's home. He parked on the street and walked over to the expedition which held Ida's dead body. It was now close to 3'oclock in the morning and the job was almost done. Tony got inside the car and drove to Mathews home. He first drove by the home slowly before turning around. Mathew had parked the Chrysler on the street as he'd always done instead of putting it in the garage. Tony pulled up behind Matthews car, popped the trunk took one last look around and put Ida's body in the trunk and close the lid. Tony looked up at Mathew's windows and was positive that no one was watching. Tony got back into the expedition, started it and left.

CHAPTER 5 - THE INCIDENT

Taya got out of the shower and walked over to the bathroom mirror while drying her shoulder length hair. She yelled at Mark who was downstairs and who she had hopped was starting a strong pot of coffee. Taya wrapped her head with the towel and pulled another one down from the rack, to wrap around her body.

"Mark!" Taya yelled again.

She went over to the dresser, opened the drawer and slipped on a pair of panties while keeping her towel in place. Taya exited the bedroom and walked downstairs. Taya began to yell Mark's name again when she noticed the front door was open. Taya then realized she didn't hear Max, the couples German Sheppard, and she hadn't heard the usual sounds made by Mark's normal routine. Taya backed up slowly as to not make any more sounds which could possibly alert an intruder. She went back into the bedroom and put on a pair of jeans that she left on the chair in the corner of the spacious bedroom. She also retrieved a shirt which was in the same place. Taya hurried to the night stand which was on the side of the bed and retrieved a .22 caliber smith & Wesson that she had bought years before against the wishes of her loving husband. Since Mark was against the idea of having a gun in the house, Taya had gone to the shooting range with a couple of friends that worked in the D.A.'s office. She was no expert, but she was comfortable with the weapon. Taya tiptoed over to the bedroom door, now trying to look over the railing while standing seemingly safe from her bedroom door. It was dead silent. in the home and Taya's breathing became rapid. She tried to calm herself down but was unable to. This was a fear that she always had in the back of her mind, that one day all the senseless crime that she had read so much about in hundreds of discoveries would somehow find her and shatter her peaceful existence. Taya wanted to pull out the clip to make sure it was full of ammo as she had left it, but was afraid that the sound of the clip being ejected would alert would be thieves or worst, would be killers. Taya heart was beating so loud that she was sure someone would hear her. Again she tried to calm herself as she started walking out of the bedroom and towards the stairs. She could feel her heart pumping an enormous amount of blood through her veins. She held her hand straight, with her other hand cupping both her hand and the weapon. As she started down the stairs, she could see the front door hinge was broken, now she knew without any doubt that her suspicions were not just suspicions they were reality. Taya's eyes started to tear up. Not from sadness but through pure fright. She was now breathing even heavier than before but she knew she had to keep going. She knew she had too – not for herself but for her husband – she had to find Mark.

Chapter 6 – The Dream

Carla walked off the bus started to walk towards Tony smiling. Tony returned the smile to Carla. She was truly beautiful both inside and out. Tony couldn't understand Carla's heart. She was the type of person that if she was short changed at a store she would never say anything because she didn't want the clerk to feel like they'd done something wrong. She was by far the kindness woman Tony had ever met. And with her, he felt kinder and more compassionate.

"You look great." Tony said with a smile.

"Thank you, you look pretty good yourself, Mister." Carla replied back as she placed her arms around Tony's shoulders and kisses him. Tony puts his hands on her face and kisses her back.

"Wow! That was a pretty good kiss. What was that for? Oh my God we're in public too?" Carla exclaimed sarcastically.

"Yeah, yeah yeah." Tony replied.

"So what movie are we seeing?" Carla asked.

"I say we get back on the bus. Go to my house and bake some muffins or something." Tony stated with a sly grin.

"No, Tony. We bake more muffins then anyone I know. No sir. We are going to the movies and we can bake muffins later." Carla said while pulling Tony in the direction of the theatre. The two walked up to the ticket counter

"Two for Die Hard, please." Tony stated. Tony and Carla walk over to the concession stand, to get pop corn and a soda to share. Tony grabs the change and he and Carla start walking towards the theater.

"Alright Car. I am going to show you the secret to eating popcorn." Tony states.

"Oh yeah…there's a secret?"

"Of course." Tony stops and sticks his tongue out, presses it against a kernel and pulls it into his mouth.

"Oh my…I'm not doing that."

"Come on just try it." Tony says while putting the cup of popcorn to Carla's mouth. Carla sticks out her tongue, but draws back nothing.

"Come on, Tony, the movie about to start." Carla says while laughing.

"Not until you do the popcorn tongue grab", Tony says, "Now c'mon and stick that tongue out."

"Alright, all right." Carla says. She sticks out her tongue and two kernels cling to it as she pulls them into her mouth. "I DID IT!!! I DID IT!" Carla yells. Tony becomes quiet. and stares at the popcorn, with a serious look.

"What?" Carla asks.

"Nothing, Car, I just don't want you putting germs into my popcorn."

"Shut up." Carl says as she punches him in the arm. "You told me to do it." Tony begins to laugh, "I know I told you to do it, but I didn't say lick every kernel in the cup."

Carla pokes her bottom lip out as if to show shame with a smile. Tony places his arm around her. "Just kidding…baby. You did great!"

"Was I really?"

"Yep." Just like one of those Budweiser frogs."

"Keep going with smart comments Mister and you won't be baking muffins for quite awhile."

"What I meant sweetie was that was outstanding! If eating pop corn was an Olympic sport, you would have gotten all ten's." Tony stated, trying to get back in good graces. Carla smiles and walks into the theatre. As she enters, the doors shut behind her leaving Tony in the lobby. Tony looks around; there is no one else in the theatre. The concession stand that he was just at is abandoned. Carla is gone. Tony is alone with silence. In the distance of the lobby's main corridor a man appears, walking towards Tony. Tony squints in an attempt to make out the face of the man walking towards him. He knows the walk but can't identify the dark figure.

As it comes closer into view Tony realizes, it's a man. – An older version of Tony himself. Tony goes pale as his future self stands within a forearms length before him.

"Who are you?" Tony asks.

At that moment following the words whispered from Tony's lips, everything about him dissipates, into a barely tangible vapor, dark color. But the man, now in black, remains staring directly at Tony. Everything is gone - no more…including Carla.

"Sleeping is a waste of time." whispered the man in black, "and you have things to do."

Tony opened his eyes and found himself lying in his own bed. It seemed as if the dreams of his past were becoming more frequent. And he didn't understand. Was his memory finally coming back or was his mind playing tricks on him.

CHAPTER 7 - SHOCK

Taya looked at the steps that she was trying her best to quietly tiptoe down. She was having difficulty breathing now and the Smith & Wesson silver hand gun that when she brought it she had thought it was very small and light now felt like a dumbbell in her hands. Taya tried peering over the rail as she continued her decent. Fear kept her taking a full look but it was also fear that kept her going. Taya didn't know what a heart attack felt like but she felt as if she was having one but still continued down. as she reach the floor she straighten the arm the gun was in still cupping the handle of the gun with her other hand as she was taught. As she stood by the damaged door Taya thought for a second about running out as fast as she could to try and summon help but as she looked past the living room into the kitchen she could see blood on the white linoleum floor. Taya still could hear no sound coming from anywhere in the house. Or maybe her heavy breathing masked all that could be heard. She thought about calling out her husband's name, but didn't want a possible intruder to know her position. She looked around the living room and there was nothing out of place and no place for anyone to hide. Whoever had broken in was not in the living room, she felt with everything she had that the intruder was in the kitchen awaiting her arrival. Taya walked closer to the kitchen and now noticed what looked like a little blood was an actual pool of blood. Her heart sank inside her chest. She was now breathing even heavier than before and tears continued to flow form her eyes, not from fear but from thinking whose blood it was. Taya's hands started shaking uncontrollably, as hard as she tried to steady them. she noticed the opened sliding door through the kitchen from where she stood almost at the door way of both living room and kitchen. Taya now stood straight up against the wall. She was not going to sneak around anymore. It was time to fight. Not time to be a victim. She was going to kill whoever had violated her and Mark's home. Taya charged into the kitchen, saw no one. No one but Mark lying in a pool of his own blood. He was naked, lying on his stomach. Taya dropped the gun and hurried over to him

"MARK!!"

She turned him over onto his back found that his stomach had been cut open so much that the blood was black.

"MARK!! Oh God Nooo!!!" Taya screamed, as she searched Mark's neck for a pulse. Taya got up and ran for the phone on the kitchen table. She dialed 9-1-1. Taya took her shirt off and tried to apply pressure to the four inch cut. Taya looked at Mark's face. It was totally lifeless.

"No!!! God No!! Mark C'mon Baby...Come on please Mark. You can't."

Taya could hear the 911 operator speaking into the phone which lay beside her. She kept rubbing Mark's hair and crying "Mark." she let out a blood curdling scream,

CHAPTER 8 – FAMILY MATTERS

Tony didn't understand why he sat in his black Lexus parked in the parking lot across form the Philadelphia Stock Exchange. He had been parked there for just about two hours watching the front door. The dream from the other night bothered him and he was not use to being bothered. Brain damage had turned him into the perfect killer but it had also taken him away from those who cared about him as he watched the doors on 19th street, his cell phone rang.

"Tony?" a male voice asked.

"Year?" Tony replied.

"The money was deposited this morning." It was Joe Mr. Casternia's right hand.

"Anything else?" Tony asked plainly

"No…Oh yea. Mr. Casternia wanted to know if you were coming to the party this weekend?"

Tony press end call on his cell phone. Joe was a good right hand but always so talkative, and that was not a good habit to have in their profession. Tony continued to study the front door of the Exchange Building. Tony leaned to the right with his arm bent on the arm rest and his right two fingers brushing the eyebrow of his right eye. As he did, he thought of the dream or memory form a couple of nights before. It was of him being 13 years old and sitting in front of the TV. Claudette and Taya walks in with groceries.

"Tony. wait until you see what I made mom buy you." Taya said grinning.

"What is?" Tony asked as he jumped up from the floor.

"Come on." Taya replied, while motioning to Tony to follow her and mom to the kitchen.

"What is it?" Tony asked again.

Taya put the bags on the kitchen table and started to look through them until she found the item and hid it behind her back.

"Come on Taya – let me see." Tony asked with excitement in his voice.

"Alright, alright."Taya, responded as she brought the surprise from hiding. "Butter Almond." It was a half gallon box of ice cream.

"Butter almond!" Tony said with excitement, snatching the tub from his sister's hand.

"Yep."

"Thank you Taya." Tony said with a huge smile on his face.

Tony continued to stroke his eyebrow as he remembered the dream. Something was changing inside of him and he wasn't sure if he liked it or not. Having no memory freed him in a lot of ways. He was always free from guilt and love and hate after the fall, his life changed. The fall had taken him away from his family and the love of his life. As he sat there he tried to understand what it was that made people hold hands with one another. What makes a person argue with another? What made them even care? Tony felt the need to get answers to questions he never asked before. As Tony went deeper into thought he saw a woman come out of the Stock Exchange front door. Her hair was shorter now, slightly above the shoulders. She walked out of talking to two other women all wearing dress suits. She was very beautiful, and looked though life had been kind to her. It was Carla, the woman he once loved. It had been years since he walked out on everyone's life. He had gotten to the point where his being around caused them more pain then not being there. Carla now stood across the street. Not two hundred feet from where Tony sat. She laughed with her acquaintances as she walked. He wondered how she had been and what experiences she gotten from life. Tony opened the car door. And his goal was to talk to her and possibly get answers to the dreams. Before he could close the car door he heard his cell phone ring from the passenger's seat. For a second he thought about just letting it ring. But decided to answer it. Tony got back in to the drivers seat and answered the phone while keeping Carla in his sights.

"Tony?" the voice asked.

"Yeah." Tony said plainly.

"TONY?" the voice questioned. It was female.

"Yeah. Who is this?"

"It's your mother."

"Claudette?"

Her voice sounded disturbed and shaky. It sounded as if something was very wrong. When he left all those years ago, Tony felt really good about leaving a number to contact, in case of an emergency. After awhile she stopped calling – not calling as often as she had in the past

"Tony. your sister needs you."

As Tony listened, his eyes watched Carla walk across the street and he followed her with eyes, until she disappeared into the crowd. Tony would not be seeing her today; instead he was going to Bethlehem.

Chapter 9 – The Martins

Tony had been driving for two hours on I 80 West on his way to his destination. He had never heard of The Confederate Knights, the hate group Claudette had just told him about not Patrick or Monica Martin, but he was drawn to the situation out of loyalty. He didn't remember much about Claudette or Taya. But the memories he had were all he needed to assist them in their plight. There were so many of them and they were so beautiful. He spent his whole life in Philly where everything was old, dirty and congested with people always in a rush. But just one hour outside the city everything was quiet and peaceful looking. Tony could not stop the thoughts of Carla. In the years after his accident had not been the type of person to reminisce, but found himself thinking about her. If the dreams were truly memories then he did have a life with her once before, not that he had doubted this fact because he had been told a million times in the months after his fall. But this is the first time he began to feel it instead of being expected to feel something he didn't. He looked at the trees and remembered something else. It was years ago and he and Carla had gone for a walk together in the neighborhood. They were heading to the park.

"You can't beat me, Car!" Tony shouted with a smile.

"Whatever, just because you're quick in the ring, doesn't mean you're just as quick running." Carla said.

"Car – I can one leg in a sling and still beat you!"

"You're conceited. I swear."

"It' not conceit if it's true."

"Prove it." Carla says as she steps at a line on the sidewalk. Tony goes to the line and they both knee down as if they were on the track.

"To the sign at the park." Carla says.

"Alright" Tony replied, with confidence.

"On your mark, get set"

"Go!" Carla yelled.

The pair took off running towards the sign in the park. Carla was a lot quicker than Tony expected and was a full two feet ahead of Tony. Carla had gotten to the sign first with Tony no more than a half a second behind.

"I had to let you win babe."

"Oh what ever!" Carla yelled while jumping playfully on Tony's back.

""I'm serious; I didn't want to put you in a bad mood for the rest of the day. Carla put her arm around Tony's neck putting him in a head lock.

"Tell the truth!" Carla said while applying pressure Tony fell to his knees. Trying to grab her arm from around his neck.

"Tell the truth and I'll let you go." Carla said laughing.

"Fine – you won!! You won!!" Tony said smiling.

Carla let go of Tony's neck and stood up. She puts out her hand as to help him up too. Tony pushes her hand away playfully and stands up with her assistance.

"Oh now you want to be nice." Tony asks.

"Hey I wasn't the only one talking smack." Carla says slyly.

"Well I would have won if my knee wasn't still hurting from that fight the other night."

"I know baby." Carla said with a smile.

"Your right." Carla responded with sarcasm in her voice.

Tony remembered a real memory not sleeping and dreaming but something that had occurred. Tony smiled as he remembered not sleeping and dreaming, but something that had happened. Tony smiled and remembered the race and looked in the rearview mirror of the car starring at his reflection. It was not very often that he smiled or laughed. Tony saw a rest area exit coming up in a mile and he decided this would be the perfect time to run a background check on the Martin's, especially since he was so close to Bethlehem, as Tony pulled into the rest area, he noticed how clean everything was. Philly was such a dirty place with dirty people to match. Even the rest areas just outside of Philly were unkempt and uncared for. As he parked, he retrieved his laptop from behind the seat, connected his modem and began his investigation. Tony noticed that the address for both Monica and Patrick were the same and after putting his address into his GPS, he found that he was about 12 miles away. He decided to go through the rest of the report, which contained known associates later. Tony got out of the car, went to his trunk, opened it and retrieved a suit case; he closed the trunk and put his suitcase on top of it. He opened it. He pulled out black long sleeve shirt, black military pants and black boots. It was close to sundown and he wanted to change clothes here so he did not have to do it in the car. Tony then went into the bathroom, relieved himself and changed into the all black attire. He was now ready. He wondered as he got back into the car if he would be lucky enough to find the home that Patrick and Monica shared unoccupied giving him time to break in, and search their home, as well as plant listening devices. This device was one of the tools used in Tony's trade. It was a great way to get both black mail material and leverage for most situations. As Tony got closer to the Martin's home, he contemplated just killing the Martin's, taking the bodies and their car and making them disappear, but would have to learn more about them before taking this plan of action. Tony began driving slower as the GPS informed him he had arrived at his destination. He looked at the home and checked to see if his luck was holding out. There was no car, he was not sure about how long he had before anyone returned to the home, but he knew that he would use whatever time he had wisely.

CHAPTER 10

Patrick paced back and forth inside his constantly under construction home which sat on about two acres of land just outside of Bethlehem, from the outside the home looked like a quaint medium size home, which was in bad need of yard work. In the driveway sat old cabinets and an even older refrigerator. The grass was brownish and somewhat of an off green color. It stood up a good foot higher than the grass the neighbors had. Patrick's neighbors could not see from Patrick's porch because of the trees and bushes. The neighboring homes were all well cared for with green manicured grass and well trimmed shrubs. Inside this home there was no furniture in the living room only rolled up old carpet, sawdust and tools. Patrick reached into his pants leg pocket and drew a pack of Marlboro cigarettes. Pat you've got to calm down Monica stated coming out of the bedroom of the range townhouse. That's easy for you to say, I've got this dead nigger and now some God dammed wetback murders hanging over my head! Patrick yelled. Hey, you're not the only one, Monica stated. Well is he coming over or what, Patrick asked, completely ignoring Monica. Yea, he says he's on his way. I can't go back to jail and I won't. Nobody's going back to jail Pat, so just relax. You weren't even involved in the wetback killing. What the fuck you talking about. I still knew it was going to happen, Patrick said while taking another puff from his lit cigarette. This shit is getting out of control. I should have cut this damn thing off and leave Patrick said, while motioning to the track device attached to his right leg. Monica walked over to Patrick and stood in front of him as if to stop him from constantly pacing. She casually takes the cigarette from his hand and takes a brief puff. You are asking as if this was the first time we have tried to rid this country of niggers. No, this is the first time we've took it this far Monica. That guy's wife is the fucking DA. Don't you get it? This is some serious shit and I know the Knights can't be backing this shit up. They are hun. How the fuck do you know that nobody's taking my calls, every thing that I've ever done has been for the brotherhood, and when I need from them the most, where are they? Monica turns around and starts to walk back to the bedroom. Where the fuck are you going? I'm just tired of this coward shit. I'm going to watch some TV until he gets here. Who the fuck are you calling a coward, you fucking whore. I should smack you in your fucking mouth. You do and I swear I will stab you right in your coward heart Monica said back to him. Patrick threw his cigarette and stepped on it and charged toward Monica. Monica reached into her pocket and pulled a switch blade. Patrick grabs her hand with the knife and pulls her hair with the other hand. Monica punches him with her free hand and kicks him in the groin. It puts Patrick on the floor screaming and grabbing his tentacles with both hands. Monica then jumps on top of Patrick and redirects the knife toward Patrick's throat. You put your hands on me again and it will be the last time you touch anything again Monica .Before Monica could finish there was a knock at the door of the house. She stood up and looked down at Patrick who was still lying in pain from the groin kick. You better be thanking God right now you fucking fagot Monica shouted in anger. She walks to the kitchen and walks back to the living room. The visitor follows her to the living room with a six pack of Budweiser beer in his arms. He sees Patrick lying on his side clutching his privates with both hands. Dam, did I come at a bad time he asked? No we just had to get something straight said Monica. Are you okay, the man asked while looking down at Patrick? Patrick arises to his knees and starts to stand up. Yea, I'm fine Patrick states while giving Monica a nasty look. Well here, the man pulls a beer off the six pack and hands it to Patrick. Patrick opens and begins to guzzle it down. Monica walks into the bedroom and Patrick walks into the kitchen and sits down at the cluttered table with his beer. So what's next Bobby Ray, Patrick says. Bobby sits down next to Patrick and puts the beers on the table. Well first we need you to keep your head and try to keep calm and try to calm down every thing, it's going to be alright, Bobby stated. This is fucking stressful, Bobby. I know. Patrick finishes his beer and grabs for another one from the now five-pack. Bobby watches as Patrick opens another beer and begins to drink it. Pat we have a problem Bobby says plainly. You don't know how to relax and keep your mouth shut. I know Bobby, it's just hard. Patrick puts the half finished beer down on the table. He starts to feel real dizzy. He tries to stand up but can't and ends up on a fall. What's going on Patrick says sluggishly, Bobby stands up, looks and Patrick loosing consciousness on the kitchen floor. What's going on is you've become a liability that we can't afford anymore. Monica comes out of the bedroom and into the kitchen and puts her hand around Bobby's waist from behind. Sorry, he was getting on my last nerve. I know baby, Bobby states while turning around to face Monica. He puts his arms over her shoulders and kisses her. Everything is going to be fine Bobby states. Patrick closes his eyes and passes out while Bobby and Monica continue their embrace over his now lifeless body.

Chapter 11- Saying Goodbye

Taya sat on the bed starring out the window. Her black pant suit was on the chair in front of her. She wanted to get up and shower, but she couldn't move. Mark, her husband, has been the gentlest kindhearted man she had ever met. She had never met anyone so honest and unassuming. He was her one true love, and on this day, she was going to have to put him the ground. Taya couldn't even sit anymore. Tears wield up in her eyes and she began to sob once as she had done every day for the past week since her husband's life was taken. Taya felt as if her life was over and tried to make some since of everything that has happened. She had never been the type to just give up, but she found herself doing just that. Since the day of Mark's death, food had no taste; the days had no smells or colors. As she sat on her knees crying, she looked at a sock partially showing under the bed that belonged to Mark, and she remembered constantly telling Mark to put his socks inside the laundry basket, something he always tried to do, but never did. Taya picked up the sock and smelled it. She thought about how cold his feet were at night and how often he would try to warm them by rubbing them against hers. She remembered how upset she would get with him, and now it seemed so pointless a thing to get upset with. Taya pulled the sock from where it laid and began to smell it as she squeezed it with both hands. It stilled smelled of Mark and it gave her comfort. There was a little soft knock at the door, but she didn't here it. She was deep into her thoughts, deep into her memories. It was her mother who had on a black dress which contoured to her small thin body. She walked over to Taya who was kneeling and gripping a piece of her husband's clothing. Sweetie, are you okay? Claudette asked as she gently put her hand on Taya's back and rubbed it. Taya began to cry more and more as she began to speak, but could only shake her head to answer her mother's question. Claudette also kneeled by her distraught daughter and began to hug her. It's okay baby, just let it all out, let it all out. I just don't know what to do next mom. Taya said while stuttering her shoulders feel as if her body was giving up. Baby you know what you need to do next is you live, you live for both yourself and Mark because he would not want you to give up and neither do I Claudette said, while cuddling her adult child. I never thought this would be so hard, I could barely breath and I just feel so week Mom. I know meha, Claudette states in English and half Spanish. It will get better, I promise. Just allow yourself to mourn, allow yourself to feel what you feel my daughter. The two women continued to hold each other and comfort each other. The car is outside and ready to take us to the church Claudette said. Okay, Taya said, while trying to gain her composure. Claudette gets up and goes to the bathroom and grabs some tissue. She gave the box to Taya. Take your time, meha. I will tell him to wait. Thanks mom, Taya states while accepting the tissues as she begins to dry her tears. I'll be right down, Taya said. Claudette goes out of the room and gently closes the door. Taya looks at Mark's sock once again and puts it on her cheek. I love you Mark, she states as she begins to stand. She walks over to the chair that held her clothes. This was to be filled with tears of sadness, but right now she needed to get dressed and she needed to lay her husband's body to rest.

CHAPTER 12 – BREAKING AND ENTERING

It was 2:00 p.m. and Tony had been parked up the road from where the Martin's home was. He was far enough away not to be notice by them, but close enough to see their home with his binoculars. Tony could only stare at the background report, looking at the common associate list on both Monica and Patrick's reports....Robert Ray. Tony wasn't sure if it was the same Robert Ray responsible for his accident until he observed him getting out of his green F150 and entered the Martin's home. Just seeing him angered Tony. He had no memory of the events that led up to the events of him being pushed out of Bobby's apartment window years ago. But had been told of the story a few times by Taya. Troy had starred at the picture given to him of Bobby, a picture that Tony had looked at for weeks, it was as if Tony was trying to burn Bobby's image into his mind and it worked. Bobby looked older, but still the same clean shaven guy he was when this picture was taken all those years ago. Tony had planned to end Bobby's life years before when he first started working for the mafia, but wasn't sure at the time that he would be the prime suspect. So he decided to wait a few more years, but I guess destiny has a mind of its own. As Tony put the binoculars up to his eyes, he continued with his thoughts of vengeance when he observed both Monica Martin and Bobby Ray coming out of the Martin's home and entering Bobby's F150. Tony thought aloud in a subtle whisper now where are you two going and where is your husband Monica. Troy watched as the two got into the truck and drove off. Tony put the binoculars back into the vehicle of his car. He knew he needed to get back into the house. Now that he knew the lay out inside he knew it would be easier to move around within the house. He looked outside of his car windows surveying the neighborhood. Tony needed to be perfect, it was his trademark, perfection. Through the years since he first left his mother's home and started contracting for the mob, he had truly been perfect methodical in his planning. This reputation made him the highest paid set up man in the business. But it didn't come without sacrifices. He would never forget the pain he caused his mother or Taya. He will never forget Carla and how hard she fought to hold on to a love he didn't remember. He still felt that he had done the best thing for everyone in leaving. He knew he could never be the man they remembered. Leaving his loved ones was difficult, but it had to be done. Tony reached inside his glove compartment and grabbed his 9mm glock and belt clip and set it on his waste and exited the car. He was still wearing a black t shirt and black cargo pants. He knew that if he was spotted by anyone, then calling the police would be the first thing a person would do after seeing Tony sneaking around and wearing that getup. While Tony had no idea how long he would be around or inside the Martin's home, and if it turned out he was going to be there well into the night then the black he was wearing would have been perfect. Tony made it to the storage shed unseen and unheard. As he kneeled he reached into his pants pocket and retrieved a pair of second skin black gloves and put them on. Tony again surveyed the neighborhood as he made his approach to the home. Patrick's car was still parked outside. As Tony peaked through the opening window at the side of the home, he thought to himself, that this would actually be a great opportunity for the setup. He would go in carefully, not disturbing anything, kill Patrick, take his body and make him responsible for the havoc that would follow as Tony looked through the window, he could see nothing out of the ordinary in the living room nor could he hear any movement coming from the house. Tony decided to move to the back of the home where he had entered before. He turned the doorknob slowly and gave it just enough torque to find out if it was locked. He reached into his cargo pants leg once again, this time pulling out his lock pick set; he opened it and began to pick the lock to the door which led to the kitchen. Tony heard a click, but it did not come from the door handle, it was the sound of a gun being cocked. Don't move, and turn around slowly. It was a voice of a woman, probably in her 30's. Maybe Monica had returned and Tony was just too distracted by trying to pick the lock. Either way, he had to be quick in disarming her and quiet so as to not alarm the neighbors or Patrick from inside the house. Tony put the tools down and raised his hands slowly. He wasn't sure how much distance there was between him and the would-be shooter, so he decided to take a chance that she would not shoot him before he had a chance to turn and face her. Someone who wanted him dead would have shot first and asked questions later. So it was obvious that this person wanted answers. If you even blink there will be brains all over that door you are trying to break into. Now turn around and slow the female voice said forcefully. As Tony turned he prepared for his attack. Tony? It was his sister Taya, his twin sister. What the hell are you doing here? I can ask you the same question, Tony replied. I came by to talk to the people who live in this house. Since when does a DA come by a person's house that she's prosecuting? Oh, I guess it's only ok when a mafia hit man is breaking and entering huh? She asked sarcastically. I am not a mafia hit man Tony stated. Yea, then what are you Tony, and what are you doing here? Tony starred at Taya with a blank look as though she never asked the question. Taya shook her head as she put her gun back in her Channel hand bag never mind, I don't know why I even bother asking you a question like that. It's like talking to a brick wall. Actually bricks show more emotion. Tony again remained quiet. Well it's good to see some things never change. Tony again remained quiet. Taya bends over and picks up Tony's lock pick set off the ground, hands it to Tony. Here's an idea, have you ever thought about knocking on the door? Again, Tony had no response to Taya's sarcasm. You know I could have you thrown in jail right now for what I just saw Taya said as she waited for an answer to her knock. But let me guess, your going to give me a break right? Tony asked. And that would only be because your not out here with the authority of the DA's office are you? Tony stated with the same amount of sarcasm that Taya just displayed. Well are you going to open the door or just stand there asking more questions Taya said to Tony. Tony opened the door. Wait here Tony said as he pulled the gun from his holster. "Are you freaking kidding me?" I don't need protecting Tony. Besides, I have more rights to enter this house than you do Taya said sharply. Oh, sorry, Tony said while clearing the way for Tony for Taya to get in front of him. Oh, I forgot that the assistant DA could enter anyone's property that they wanted to Tony said sarcastically under his breath. "What was that"? Taya asked. Nothing, after you Tony said while motioning as if inviting her in. Taya pulled her gun out of her bag and placed the bag by the door before entering the house. Hello, Taya said while pushing open the country style door. Taya went further into the doorway and could see black cowboy boots and blue jeans and white shirt. She walked in further and could clearly see, it was Patrick Martin his eyes were opened, but she could not see if he was breathing. The sight of Patrick laying there lifeless brought back memories of her husband. She now realized that this was harder than she originally thought. Tony walked in behind her and also saw Patrick lying on the kitchen floor. Tony looked around the body slowly searching for clues. He looked over the table that was inches away from Patrick's body. Tony walked over to the table and picked up the beer can and smelled it. What are you doing Taya asked? Succinylcholine, Tony said. "What is it"? Tony asked. It's an odorless tasteless drug and its how he died Tony proclaimed. Tony then walked over to the curtains on the window located in the kitchen and reached inside the seam and pulled out his button camera. Tony knew the drug well. He actually used it a few times himself, but decided against telling Taya about that part of the story. What's that Taya asked? Tony looked at the camera before putting it in his pocket and said a guilty verdict.

Chapter 13 – The Plan

Bobby and Monica sat at a booth in a dimly lit restaurant and bar the two had their drinks and were waiting the dinner they ordered. Monica sat starring at her beer that she was drinking straight from the bottle. What's the matter M? Okay Monica licked up her beer and looked at Bobby with a complex look. I don't know I just didn't expect you to kill him today. Monica looked around as if she now realized where she had just made the statement. She lowered her tune. I mean, I knew we were going to, I just didn't expect you to do it so soon, Monica stated bluntly. Babe listen, it doesn't make a difference whether it was today or next month, the plan is still the same. I will take care of Pat's body and he'll look like he took off to avoid prosecution for ADA's husbands. Hell, I should even go back to Taya's home and kill that fucking cunt too, and make it look like Patrick did her ass too. Bobby stated angrily. Do you still love her or something? Why would you ask that Bobby asked? Because you get so angry when you talk about her. "Shut the fuck up"! Bobby stated starring intently at Monica. You going to make me, Monica asked. Monica pulled the stainless steel butter knife off of the table slowly, carefully, as to not alert Bobby that she now had a weapon. Bobby who was sitting across from Monica was now sliding over closer to her while still staring at her. Monica gripped the knife tightly and prepared herself for the worst. Bobby got over to Monica looked around to see if anyone was looking over he was sure no one was looking he spoke. You need to remember who the fuck your talking to, I am not your husband, he's dead you ever talk that shit to me again and you will need more than that fucking knife. Monica leaned closer to Bobby. All I am saying is that if you want to go back to your spick ex-girlfriend then go. And you might do well to remember that I don't respond well to threats. If we have a problem just let me know. Bobby looked at Monica and she looked back at him. He knew that Monica didn't fear anything and also knew that she was not above making a scene whether it was at a restaurant or a church she didn't care. No, we have no problems babe, Bobby stated while giving Monica a kiss on the lips. Let's stop this fighting shit okay. Okay Bobby, Monica says, as she kisses Bobby back. Monica takes the knife from her hand and places it back on the table where she got it from. So what's next, Monica asked? Well let's eat and then back to the house. Well let's eat and then back to the house so you can pack some things and I will get rid of Patrick come back, pick you up and we are off to Texas. Bobby stated with confidence. And you're sure the confederates there will give us what we need? Monica asked. I'm sure it's all been arranged. The waitress comes over to the table and brings two plates of food. Bobby paid no mind to her as she did so, still only starring at Monica. Will there be anything else the waitress asked? No Monica answered rudely. The waitress rolled her eyes and only left the table in discuss and Monica and Bobby continued their kiss.

Chapter 14 - Reunion

Bobby and Monica drove up to the house, parked in the driveway, got out of the truck. Bobby parked the truck door and went to the bed of the truck to open the tool box he had back there. Monica walked to the back of the house and reached for the keys to the back door, retrieved them and locked the door she walked inside the house and looked over at Patrick's body as it laid in the same position that she left it. As Monica laid her keys down on the counter top, she was struck in the back of the head with the butt of Taya's gun. Where's Bobby, Taya asked of Tony who was peaking out of the front window. He's going through the truck Tony replied. I am taking her in Tony. I know Tony replied plainly and without emotion. Tony tossed Taya a pair of handcuffs as he continued to peak through the drapery, which covered the front window. You will need these in case she wakes up. Taya looked at her brother as she cuffed Monica's hands behind her back. I am so sorry Tony, she said. Why Tony said while still keeping an eye on Bobby. Tony could feel her in depth star and turned and looked at his sister. I have always felt that if I only would have told you to pick up earlier, if only I told you my plans of talking to Bobby, maybe you could have talked me out of it. Maybe you could have had a normal life Taya stated with sadness and sincerity in her eyes. No regrets Taya. It's not your fault. It never was. Tony said while turning to look out the window once again. Bobby's is yours. If you turn him in you turn him in. If you don't, you don't. Either way we are now even Taya said. We were never uneven Taya, Tony said while cracking a smile. Taya looked at Tony confused. For the moment she saw the brother she had always known. The sarcastic response was unmistakable. Tony pulled his gun from the holster and headed toward the back door. Taya pointed her gun toward the back door that Tony was standing behind. Taya was nervous and was breathing heavily. She had not seen Bobby since the day he had taken her brother away from her. She wanted revenge for Mark, but knew that she couldn't do what her brother could. Taya also knew she would never be able to live with that guilt. Bobby barely opened the door his hands were so full. He was carrying a green duffle bag along with a tool box. He noticed Taya immediately, but was it was too late to take off and drop everything before being shot by her

"Taya!?" Bobby said with a shocked look on his face. Tony came up behind Bobby and hit him in the back of the head with the butt of Tony's gun, knocking him out cold. Tony then put Bobby's hands behind his back and handcuffed him.

"Now what?" Taya asked.

"Now, I put Bobby back his truck and you call the police. When Monica comes to – you tell her that you never saw Bobby. She will then think that he betrayed her and probably tell you whatever you want to know about Bobby, Patrick and the Confederate Knights," Tony said calmly while dragging bobby to the back door and opening it.

"Should I even ask where you are taking him?" Tony kneeled down beside Bobby and put Bobby over his shoulder and stood him up.

"No" Tony said while going back to Bobby's truck and placed him in the passenger's seat. As Tony put the seat belt around Bobby's passed out body and closed the passenger door to the truck he saw Taya walking down the driveway from the house. She looked at Tony and pulled him in and hugged him. As Taya squeezed harder, Tony lifted his arms and hugged her back.

"I love you – and I miss you" Taya said while burying her face in Tony's chest. Tony stood uncomfortably with the show of affection and human contact. But he remembered something.

"I remember ice cream."

"What" Taya said as she took her head out of Tony's chest and looking at him.

"I remember you surprising me with ice cream" Tony said.

Taya eyes began to water and she started smiling and hugged him tighter. Tony hugged her back and walked over to the driver side of the truck.

"Call sometimes – huh?" Taya said.

"I will" Tony said has he climbs into the truck and drives off. He looks in the rear view mirror and still sees his sister standing on the driveway watching as he drives off. He didn't know, if he would see his sister again, but for the first time in a long time… he wanted to.

Chapter 15 - Reckoning

Bobby awoke sitting in the passenger seat of his truck. His hands cuffed very hard behind his back and a headache out of this world. There was no one in the driver's seat. It was dark and because of the humid mist on the windows he was unable to see where the truck was parked at or who his capture was. Bobby leaned over and rubbed his head up and down on the passenger's window in hopes of trying to look outside. It was pitch black, Bobby knew that wherever he was it was desolate. He looked out the window and saw no cars passing by, no one walking. He did see a couple of lights which looked like they lead to a path of some kind… maybe a walkway. Maybe he was in the park. Bobby could now feel his hands pulsating as if his blood and his head were now located in this hands.

Bobby looked around as if there would be a key or a tool that could help him get free, as he tried to get his eyes to focus on the task, he heard something outside of his truck. A constant scrapping of some type, as he listened more attentively, he figured it was not scrapping but digging. Bobby could see that the mist filled the passenger's window once again, so he leaned back over to clear a space from which he could look out of once again. This time he was able to see more clearly… he was at the cemetery. As Bobby continued to hear the constant digging his heart raced.

"Hey!" Bobby yelled… He could hear the digging had stopped and whoever was digging was now at the passenger door. The door opened and Bobby saw the face he hadn't expected or seen in years… Tony.

Bobby panicked and tried desperately to get over to the driver's side, trying to escape from Tony but the seat belt held him in place. "Oh God… please Tony, I'm sorry about the window thing man. I'm sorry about everything," Bobby said as Tony unlocked the seat belt and pulled Bobby out of the truck.

"Tony! Don't you fucking do this!!! Don't… you do this!" Bobby said with tears in his eyes as Tony walked him over to the shallow grave. Bobby looked down the hole and could see an opened casket with a man in a suit already inside. Tony pulled the gun from his waist.

"Plee…." Bobby said as Tony shot him in the skull. Bobby's body fell into the grave landing on top of the unknown body. Tony looked down into the grave and took two more shots at Bobby's head. Tony then walked back over to the shovel that he leaned against the truck, grabbed it and began to fill the hole. Tony had guessed by looking at the dates on the head stone and the freshly packed dirt that the Randy Riggan that was buried there was just put there two days ago. And barring no second or third autopsy's he would never be dug up again. Tony put the shovel in the back of the truck and drove out of the cemetery. He still needed to get rid of the truck and retrieve his car. Tony drove the truck as close to the Greyhound Bus Station as he could legally park. He looked around and streets were clear. He exited the truck and locked the truck and closed the door. Tony walked to the bed of the truck and retrieved the shovel. Tony walked over to the dumpster and through it in. He then took off his gloves, put them in his pocket and began the long way back to his car.

Chapter 16 - Endings/+ Beginnings

Tony sat in his black Lexus parked in the parking lot across from the Philadelphia Stock Exchange. He had been parked there for just under two hours watching the front door. He looked at his watch and knew it was just a matter of time before he would see her. As he sat, the doors to the exchange opened as if school had just let out. Tony exited the Lexus still keeping the door to the car opened and having his right foot still in the car. He thought to himself what will he say to her, what will he feel? As his thoughts raced through his head he saw Carla. She was wearing a red flowered summer dress which seemed to rest on her body effortlessly and beautifully.

Tony was about to close the car door but then the phone began to ring. It was on the passenger seat where he left it. He hesitated, thinking for a moment while he thought of what he should do. He closed the car door and walked across the street to see what destiny had in store for him now.

THE END